# Butterfly Tree

With love for Shirley Dodd

*—S. M.*

To my mother and daughter

*—L. W.*

# Butterfly Tree

Sandra Markle
Illustrated by Leslie Wu

PEACHTREE
ATLANTA

It's late afternoon in early September.
I'm playing fetch on the beach with Fudge.
I toss the stick. I stop.
Shading my eyes with my hand,
I look out over the slate gray water.

Out past the rocky point,
way out over Lake Erie,
it looks like it's raining black pepper
from a clear blue sky.

Fudge bounds back with the stick in his mouth,
but I keep on watching.

The black rain becomes a wispy mist.
Then it turns into a cloud
that grows bigger,
until it's blimp-sized.

But this cloud isn't white
or gray.
It's orange,
and it shimmers.

What in the world could it be?
Fallout from a distant volcano?
Smoke from a faraway fire?
Could it be an alien spaceship?
Or the breath of an invisible dragon?

With Fudge at my heels,
I run as fast as I can
up the path to our cabin.

Mom's packing the car.
It's nearly time to go home.
*What's happened, Jilly?*
she asks, looking worried.

*Look!* I exclaim.
Mom gasps.

I ask Mom if we should
get in the car and escape.
But she orders Fudge to stay
and heads for the beach.
*Hurry, Jilly!* she calls. *Walk on fast feet!*

The sand is soft.
Plowing through it is hard work.
So I step in Mom's footprints, which is easier,
except for when I have to take giant steps to match hers.

Not far ahead, the orange cloud
comes ashore and sinks
into the woods edging the beach.

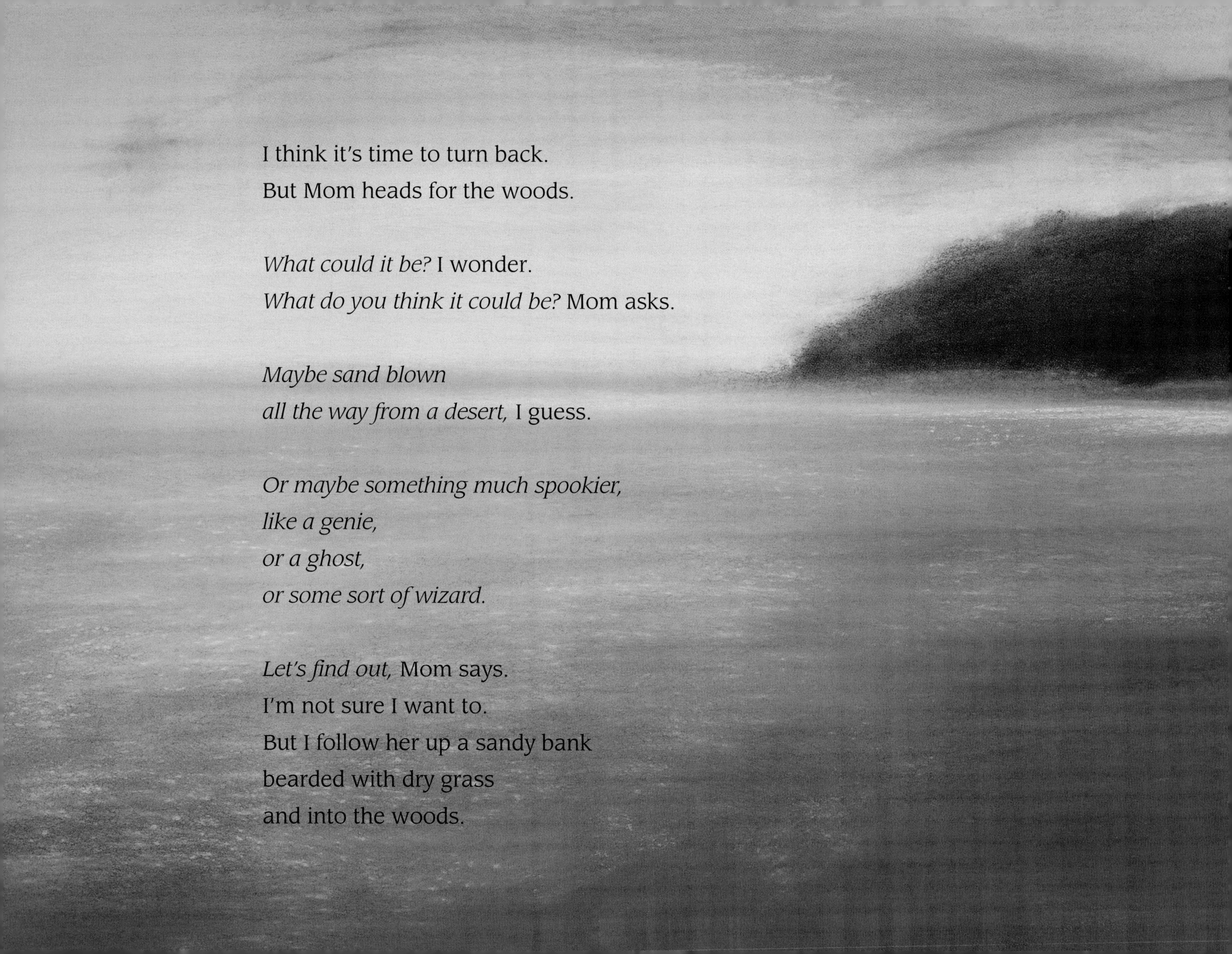

I think it's time to turn back.
But Mom heads for the woods.

*What could it be?* I wonder.
*What do you think it could be?* Mom asks.

*Maybe sand blown*
*all the way from a desert,* I guess.

*Or maybe something much spookier,*
*like a genie,*
*or a ghost,*
*or some sort of wizard.*

*Let's find out,* Mom says.
I'm not sure I want to.
But I follow her up a sandy bank
bearded with dry grass
and into the woods.

It's much cooler
and dimmer here.
My arms prickle with goose bumps
as we slip through the shadows
that knit the tall trees together.

When I hear a rustle above me, I stop and look up.
I spot something orange move.
*Mom!* I say, pointing.

She comes close.
But it's only a Baltimore oriole
looking down at us from its high perch.

*Shhh!* Mom whispers.
*Be quiet.*
*Keep looking.*

Our footsteps sound too loud.
I feel like I should tiptoe.

I look so hard I think my eyes will pop.

Then I spot something orange
in high branches just up ahead.

Is it part of the cloud?
Or a monster ready to pounce?
But it's only a wind-tattered kite
the forest has caught.

*Guess we should turn back,* I say.
But Mom points left,
where we spy golden-orange
between dark tree trunks.

But it's only a clearing
with one big, tall tree
covered in sunlit clumps
of orange leaves.

Suddenly, Fudge races past us,
barking and chasing
a squirrel up the tree.

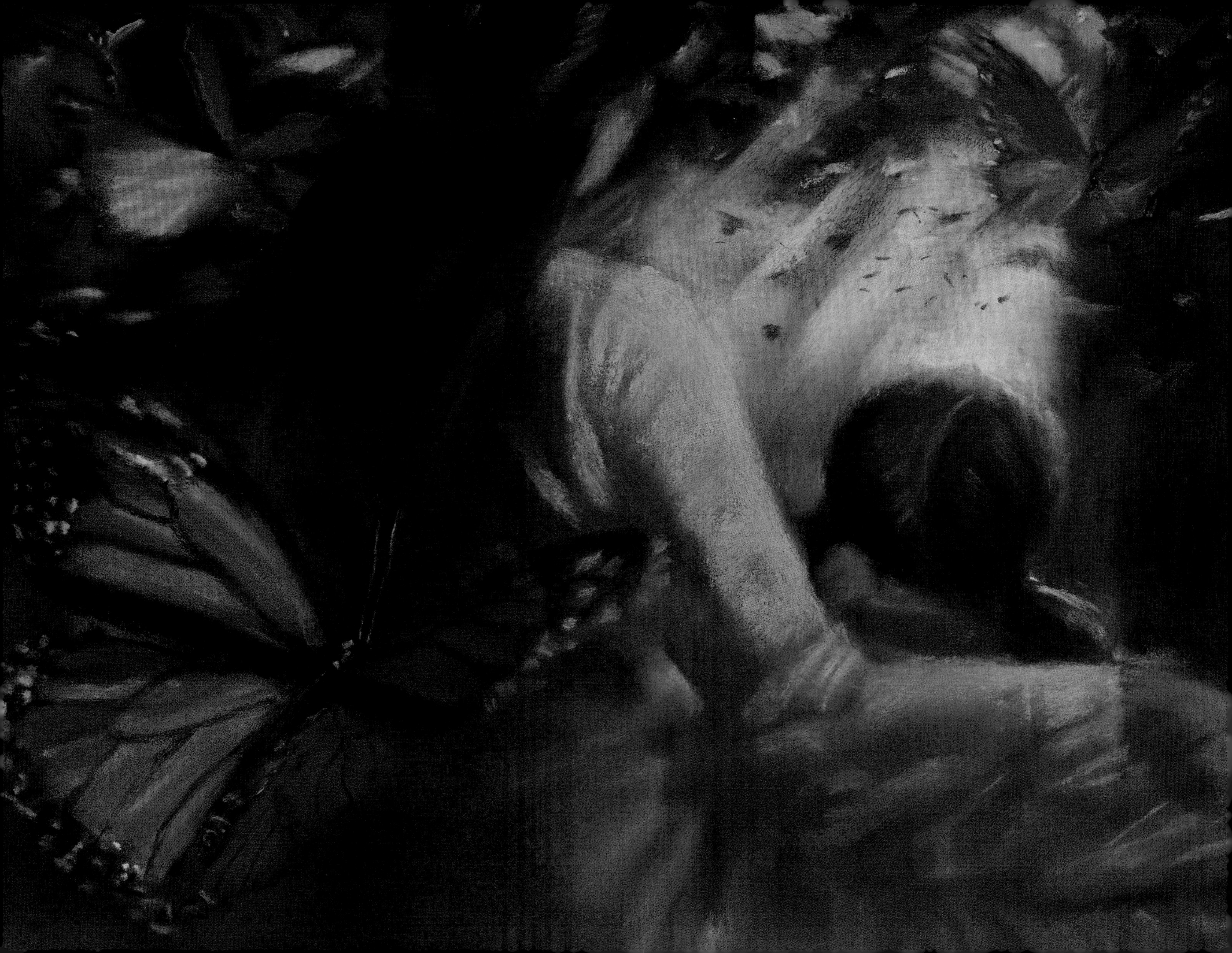

An explosion
of golden-orange bits
fills the sunlight
streaming between branches.

*Wow!* I exclaim. *They're not leaves.*
*They're butterflies.*

*Monarch butterflies,* Mom says.

There must be hundreds—thousands.
The tree looks like it is in motion.
All the butterflies are slowly fanning their wings.

We are inside an orange cloud
of still more fluttering butterflies.
A monarch perches on Mom's nose.
More land on her head.
She looks like she has butterfly hair.

She points at me, and I know
I have butterfly hair too.

One lands on Fudge's nose
but only stays 'til he jumps and barks.
Then all the butterflies are airborne again.

Mom tugs on Fudge's collar
and we leave the clearing.
But we stay in the woods, watching.
Mom tells me the monarchs are only resting
during their journey south for the winter.

The butterflies settle again
onto every branch and twig.
The big tree looks bejeweled
in the glow of the setting sun.

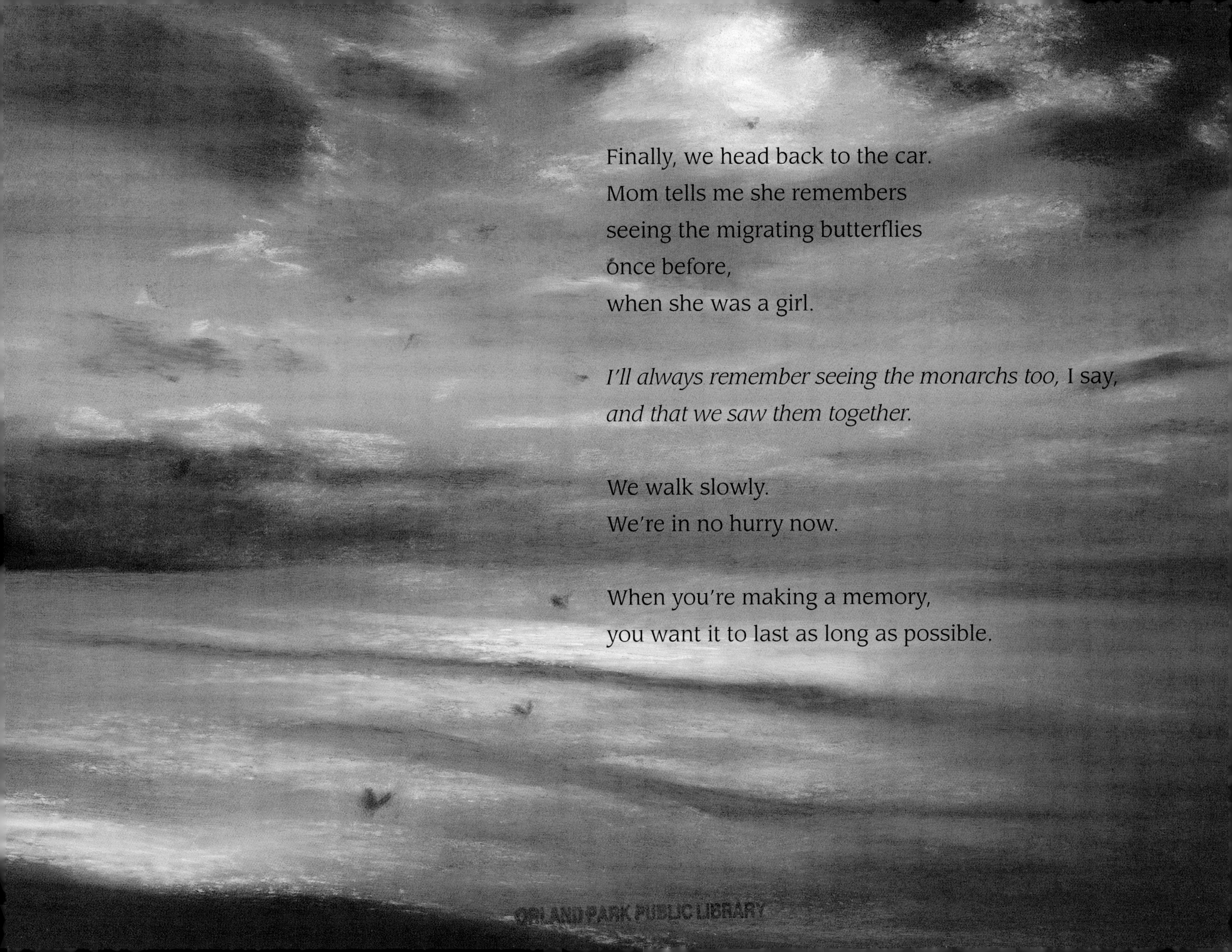

Finally, we head back to the car.
Mom tells me she remembers
seeing the migrating butterflies
once before,
when she was a girl.

*I'll always remember seeing the monarchs too,* I say,
*and that we saw them together.*

We walk slowly.
We're in no hurry now.

When you're making a memory,
you want it to last as long as possible.

# Author's Note

I GREW UP in northern Ohio, where weekends and vacations meant wonderful times on the shores of Lake Erie. For me, beautiful autumn afternoons will forever spark the memory of the day I happened to be on the beach when a migrating flock of monarchs crossed the lake and settled for the night. Their arrival at first seemed spooky—then magical. Being surrounded by these golden-orange butterflies and seeing a tree totally covered with fluttering, shimmering monarchs was unforgettable.

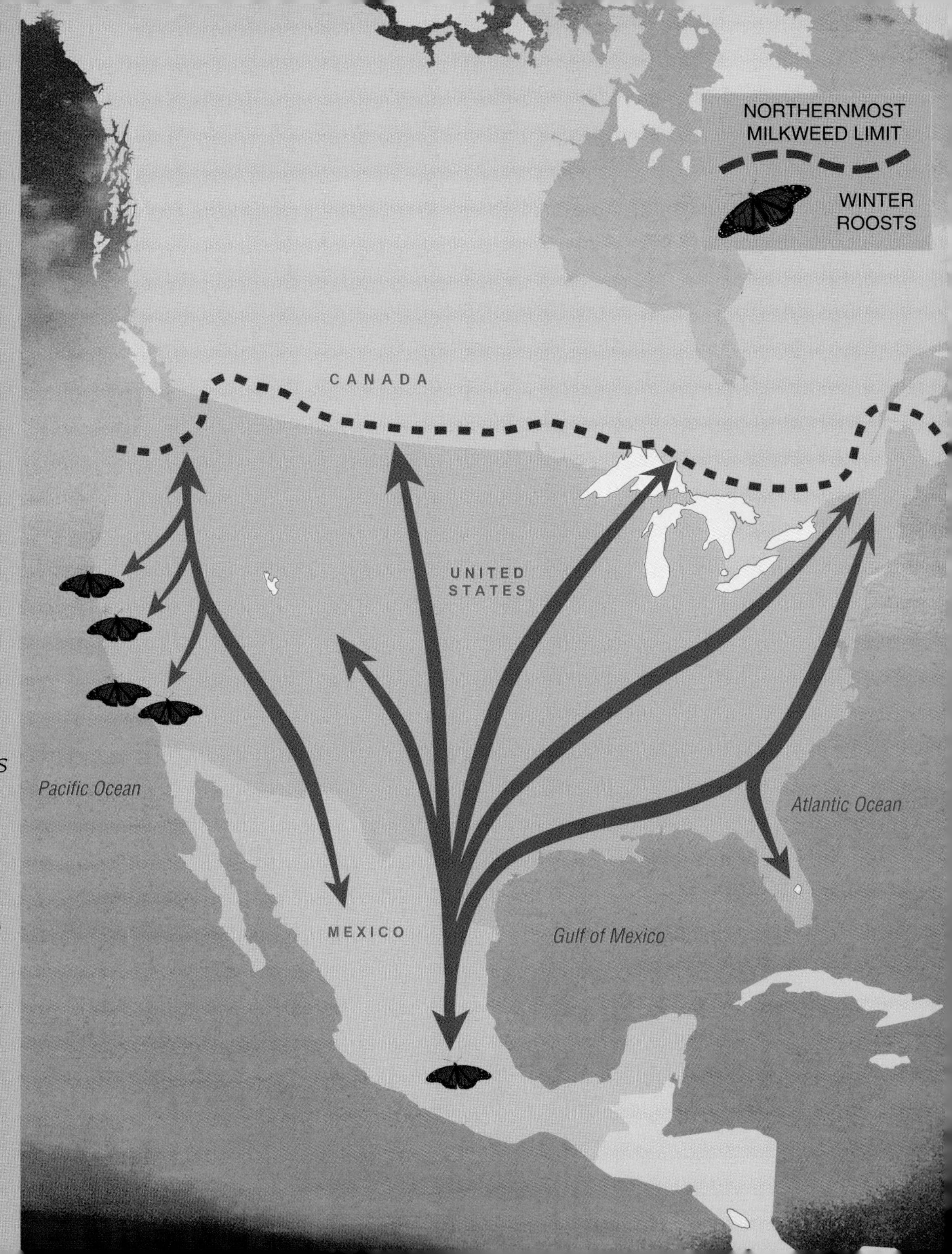

# Traveling Monarchs

MONARCHS do not fly in a flock the way birds do. Each butterfly flies alone, but it follows the same path as lots of other monarchs. So when they land to feed or rest, there may be thousands all together. The amazing journey lasts for weeks and takes the monarchs on a route they've never covered before. Monarch butterflies traveling from Canada fly as far as 2,000 miles (3,218 kilometers). Those migrating east of the Rocky Mountains winter in Mexico. Those to the west of the Rockies winter in southern California. At the end of their journey, the monarchs settle in the same forests monarchs have wintered in year after year.

Monarchs stop to feed on nectar as they migrate. If you live along their flyways, plant colorful wildflowers. Then your home may be a monarch stopover. You'll need to check with a local plant nursery for what to grow in your area. Here are some flowers monarchs especially like: sunflowers, New England asters, butterfly weed, and purple coneflowers.

# More Information

## BOOKS

**Monarch Butterflies Up Close** by Carmen Bredeson. (Enslow) Real photos let you take a close look at monarch butterflies during every stage of their life.

**Monarch Butterfly** by Gail Gibbons. (Holiday House) Learn more about these butterflies and how they live.

**Monarchs** by Kathryn Lasky. (Gulliver Books) Beautiful photos and text share the monarch butterfly's migration. Learn how people are working to protect the monarchs' winter-over homes.

**Mexico or Bust! Migration Patterns** by Deborah Underwood. (Raintree) Follow monarchs as they travel south for the winter.

## WEBSITES

**Monarch Picture Story**
*www.kidzone.ws/animals/monarch_butterfly.htm*
Have fun investigating monarchs.
Don't miss the animated jigsaw puzzles.

**Journey North's Monarch Butterfly Migration Tracking Project**
*www.learner.org/jnorth/monarch*
Get up-to-date information on migrating monarchs. Explore the site to read true stories about these butterflies, see photos, and learn lots of cool facts.

**Monarch Butterfly USA**
*www.monarchbutterflyusa.com/Cycle.htm*
See a monarch hatch on this animated site. Watch a caterpillar grow and change into its pupa stage, then see an adult emerge.

# Acknowledgments

*The author would like to thank Dr. Chip Taylor, Director of Monarch Watch (www.MonarchWatch.org), University of Kansas, and Dr. Simon Pollard, Curator of Invertebrate Zoology at Canterbury Museum, Christchurch, New Zealand, for sharing their enthusiasm and expertise.*

*A very special thank-you to Skip Jeffery for sharing the creative process.*

Published by
PEACHTREE PUBLISHERS
1700 Chattahoochee Avenue
Atlanta, Georgia 30318-2112
*www.peachtree-online.com*





Art direction by Loraine M. Joyner
Composition by Melanie McMahon Ives
Illustrations created in pastels. Title typeset in Manfred Klein's ParmaPetit-Normal; text typeset in International Typeface Corporation's Leawood Book and Korinna.

Printed in March 2011 by Tien Wah Press in Singapore
10 9 8 7 6 5 4 3 2 1
First Edition

**Library of Congress Cataloging-in-Publication Data**

Markle, Sandra.
Butterfly tree / written by Sandra Markle ; illustrated by Leslie Wu.
p. cm.
Summary: When Jilly encounters a mysterious orange cloud on a family outing to Lake Erie, she and her mother go to investigate the phenomenon. Includes facts about monarch butterflies. Includes bibliographical references.
ISBN 978-1-56145-539-3 / 1-56145-539-3
[1. Monarch butterfly--Migration--Fiction. 2. Butterflies--Fiction.] I. Wu, Leslie, ill. II. Title.
PZ7.M3396Bu 2010
[E]--dc22

2009040526